For Dan and Elizabeth,
who find dirt roads that lead to fun.

Brad and Emily's Treasure Adventure copyright © 2001 Mary Hubley

Printed in Canada
First Edition

Publisher's Cataloging-in-Publication
(Provided by Quality Books, Inc.)

Hubley, Mary.
   Brad and Emily's treasure adventure / Mary Hubley. –
1st ed.
   p. cm.
   SUMMARY: Pirates have stolen King Crab's treasure, so
Brad and Emily are off to the rescue. In a land of
talking crabs and turtles and naughty clouds, they'll
have to face the ferocious pirates—and learn something
important about cooperation.
   Audience: Pre K-2.
   LCCN 2001-116129
   ISBN 0-9707267-0-8

   1. Treasure-trove—Juvenile fiction. 2. Pirates—
Juvenile fiction. 3. Crabs—Juvenile fiction.
[1.Treasure hunts—Fiction. 2. Pirates—Fiction. 3. Crabs
—Fiction.] I. Title.

PZ7.H86345Br 2001   [E]
     QB121-83

ATTENTION SCHOOLS AND BUSINESSES
Bluefish Bay books are available at quantity discounts with bulk purchases for educational, business, or sales promotional use. For information, please write to Specialty Sales Department, Bluefish Bay Publishing, Inc., 1093 A1A Beach Blvd., PMB 148, St. Augustine, FL 32080 or at www.BluefishBay.com.

Brad and Emily's Treasure Adventure

Written and Illustrated by Mary Hubley

Bluefish Bay
Publishing, Inc.
St. Augustine, Florida

Through the dunes, Emily and Brad walk along,
Singing a spirited pirating song.
A hearty tune they can sing today,
To make them brave and scare pirates away:

"Yo ho ho, off we go!
A pirate quest, yo ho ho!
Pirates—run! Look out below!
Here we come! Yo ho ho!"

Their song attracts a crab on the beach,
The kids are shocked as it whispers a speech:

"I am King Crab, the king of the shore.
Pirates sailed here and waged a war.

They attacked last night with big swords and whips.
Then took my treasure and ran to their ships.

I'm seeking knights to find my gold chest.
Is your song true? Would you go on a quest?"

Their thrilled "Yes!" earns them royal rights,
The king gives them the title of knights.

"This map I found can show you the way;
restore my land's riches, wherever they lay."

They're excited and search every beach nook,
Emily holds up the map for a better look.

They look up in wonder; clouds start to motion.
Wind steals the map—it flies toward the ocean.

The knights chase the map; they run quickly along.
At the edge of the rocks, a trail guides them on.

The trail leads to pirates dueling with swords.
The knights hide behind bushes close to the shore.
The pirates look mean, they're loud, and smell bad.
Emily is scared. "Me, too!" says Brad.

They look at each other and run away fast,
Beyond where they see a pirate ship's mast.

"Hello! I can help!" a green turtle yells.
"Pirates fear beach creatures—even fish and seashells."
Brad asks, "How can that be? They're dangerous and mean."
The turtle says, "They aren't as brave as they seem.
Pirates run from crabs and seagulls at play.
Let's get beach friends to help scare them away."

The knights feel braver. "Let's go!" Brad shouts.
The turtle calls friends to come help them out.
Emily giggles as wild creatures swarm in,
Marching and singing, they're sure to win.

"Yo ho ho, off we go!
A pirate quest, yo ho ho!
Pirates—run! Look out below!
Here we come! Yo ho ho!"

Brad and Emily cheer as their friends march close,
The pirates run screaming, then sail down the coast.

A trail of coins shows them what's next.
They stop when they see a dune marked with an "X".

Turtles and sand crabs help dig for the treasure.
The knights find the booty, too rich to measure.

The knights are triumphant, their quest is complete.
They lay the treasure at King Crab's feet.
The king thanks them in an honored tradition:
He gives them gold for completing their mission.

The knights accept the treasure with glee,
Then wave goodbye to King Crab and the sea.

Treasure and Pirate Facts

What is pirate's treasure? In days of old, pirates stole riches from wealthy merchant ships. The most prized treasures were gold and silver coins and bars, pearls, and precious stones. Pirates also stole other things that were valuable, such as spices, pottery, medicine, and cloth.

What did pirates do with their treasure? Treasure was usually divided equally between the pirates on a ship. Coins were cut up to make small pieces. Captain Kidd buried his treasure, but most pirates spent their booty when they reached a port, and some treasure was lost at sea.

Were there different kinds of pirates? Yes. The term *Pirate* was used to describe people who attacked and robbed ships on the sea. *Privateers* were like pirates, but they were given permission by their government to capture enemy ships. *Buccaneers* were pirates and privateers who sailed in the West Indies.

When did pirates live? Pirates have been around ever since ships started sailing the high seas. Early pirates preyed on Greek and Roman ships, and Vikings attacked Europe's coast. Pirates were very active from 1500 to the mid-1800s.

- *1500-1600:* The Barbarossa brothers became famous for attacking ships on the Barbary coast in the Mediterranean Sea. English and French privateers attacked Spanish ships in the late 1500s as they carried riches across the Atlantic Ocean from the Americas. The most well-known privateers were Sir Francis Drake and Sir John Hawkins.
- *1600-1700:* This was the classic time for pirates and pirate treasure, when Sir Henry Morgan and Captain William Kidd became well known.
- *1700-1800:* Pirates such as Samuel Bellamy and Blackbeard lived during the 1700s. During the American Revolution, John Paul Jones and other privateers helped the American Navy raid English ships.
- *1800 to today:* Pirates have slowly disappeared. One reason is the invention of steam ships, which were fast enough to easily capture pirate ships. Also, an 1856 treaty, called the Declaration of Paris, led to the end of privateering in the late 1800s. Today, only a few pirates exist, living mostly in Southeast Asia and the Caribbean.

Treasure Fun and Things to do

- Study about pirates in library books, on the Web, and by visiting museums.
- Write a ship's log—a journal of how you imagine pirates spent their time.
- Make a desert island model. Use modeling clay to mold pirates, treasure, and ships.
- Create your own pirate costumes, hats, and flags.
- Draw pirate treasure maps and mazes.
- Find a book that shows pictures of pirate coins such as pieces of eight and doubloons. Copy the coins by drawing them on heavy paper and cut them out to make your own pirate treasure.
- Create and perform a play or a puppet show about pirates.
- Learn what pirates liked to eat, and make pirate food. Have a pirate party.

Need Additional Copies?

Look for additional copies of *Brad and Emily's Treasure Adventure* at your local retailer. If you cannot find them or want a personal autographed copy, you can order from the publisher directly. Call 1-866-999-BLUE toll-free or see www.BluefishBay.com for details.

More Brad and Emily Stories are Coming Soon!